Three Small Words

By

Patrick Libby

ISBN 978-0-6151-4053-7

ISBN 978-0-6151-4053-7

Thanks:
Sabrina, Jai Peruman, Michael W Dean, Henry Rollins, George Spooner, Kayla Miller, Coltrane,
Myself.

Table Of Contents

This book is not dedicated to you.

Mornings

You have no idea
the sheer magnitude

of the lies I live.
and
tell.
and
sell.
selling you a con about the inside.
my outside.
my past. my future
my head.
and my
game.
the one person that knows me
I hide from.
that last line. fucked me up.
It is the most honest I have gotten in a
long
long time.
Well, not that long.
But it hit me. as so.
or rather.
I want it to hit you. as so.

Crunch

I have
found
absolute
beauty

I will
kill myself
before
sharing it
with any
of you

1. My boyfriend beats me.

2. I am afraid drugs will kill my brother.

3. I am my grandmothers little angel.

4. I steal.

5. I cry myself awake every morning.

6. I drink before my AA meetings and tell no one.

7. I am too ashamed to eat in front of people.

8. I feel vulnerable, always.

9. My neighbor molested me when I was 8.

10. I am having another abortion.

11. I tell people I have tried to commit suicide but I never have.

12. I don't feel good enough for the ones I love.

13. My dad cheated on my mom and only I know.

14. I have not taken my psych meds in three weeks.

15. I lie to my partner about my past.

16. I am ashamed of my sexual fantasies.

All My Pens Have No Ink In Them

water spigots left rusted to drip rose colored water

(I almost do not want to continue with this)

(that is the most beautiful thing I have ever read)

(fuck, it is all downhill from here)

(on with the…)

hamper filled with garbage and crumpled paper

guitars with no strings and rotted wood

scratched cds

warped records

unwound cassettes

cigarette butts

used floss

rock hard gum on the sole of every pair of stolen shoes

un-stuffed animals

wondering how long this will go on

bridal magazines with red ink spilled onto every page

soda cans filled with dead bugs ash and dust

egg shells

dish soap

stale crackers

a box of staples

cracked knuckles

wet dreams

cash

board games with all the important pieces missing

towel with bleach spots

cancer

television

loud and oppressive talk coming from the other room

all tied off and nowhere to go

all tied up and nowhere to go

phone off hook

what
a
wonderful
world

.

Junky On The Bus

His skin is thin and yellowed,

Nails long and hard with dirt,

Hair hidden under a dirty cap,

From under his filthy long sleeves

I see home done tattoos

Untreated sores and bug bites.

His head is resting on my friends shoulder.

I know this trip.

I believe I used to ride this line to score years ago.

Dope sick and full of fear.

I ask him at what stop he is getting off

He says "7th".

I don't have it in me to tell him hes on the wrong bus.

I don't want to see that look in his eye

that says I am falling and my hands are tied.

I can remember how every bump in the road felt.

The screaming in my bones

and the broken glass in my stomach.

Today I am not him.

Not today,

Maybe tomorrow

Another Ride

I don't want my desire
or the consequences thereof

I have lived the results
the obsessions
spinning around in my own thoughts
until I become sick
ill
heaving inside

I don't appreciate my impulses
I am afraid to act
to reach out
or to accept the hands that are offered

Confusion is the one thing I understand clearly
and without doubt

I sometimes wish I was the old man on the train with
the newspaper and a wedding ring on his finger

To be completely oblivious of the young man across the aisle
with the sweat
and the fear
and obvious anger in his mouth

To not live as me anymore
To not live
Just that
to have an end

This sick fire will get me home tonight
It will raise the covers on my bed and invite me to go to sleep
to get the rest I will need to go through this all over again

It does not seem to get any easier
But,
it looks like it might make sense someday

Reason
Purpose
I wish I truly desired these things

All I want to do is jump in front of a train

I reject it only because it makes sense
and so it must be bullshit

It must
It must it must it must
It must it must

I do not have my best interest in mind

as I wrote that last line
the thing that screams at me from somewhere deep inside
yelled
"Suicide is in your best interest."

I am being attacked from within

Inaction is my only weapon
to wait it out

I wonder who will hold out longest

I guess I wont know in the end

Being In Line

When the fact that you are a sucker hits you
Man,
It's like nothing else
Warmth sliding all around the inside of your face

How fucking weak
Displaced
and
Misplaced

Again

The moment of Absolute and Harmonious
Truth is realized

I am the sucker

I always forget that
this is where
I belong

It's setting in
And I am calming down
my muscles are relaxing
I'm ok
I'm ok
I'm cooling

I am a sucker
and the truth is ok
It's ok

Anger

anger spills out of me
I spin
I walked into my room
my dogs shoulders slumped as if he was
wincing
I have never hit him
I didn't even say anything to him when I walked in
no slamming the door
I was silent
if I look at him he flinches

I don't want this anger inside me
but I get so twisted that
my tears come out hot
and burn my cheeks
I wait for them to dry and crack my skin
as I breathe
I cough
I choke on every scream
I hold inside
inflating
growing
making me sick
when I focus on the pain that my angers causes my body
I start to swell and shrink
every heartbeat
every blinking eye
is
slammed closed
and
torn open

Nothing is calm
everything is automated and violent
I sit in my chair
and watch clouds turn red over mountains
nature is disgusted by me
I am revolting
my teeth crack and become dirty dust
as I
clench my jaws closed
bite my lips off
and
spit them against the wall next to me

I force my fingers into my stomach
until I
feel my organs
they are more firm than
I
imagine them

I want to sleep
on empty
tonight
I pull my stomach and kidneys out

I put them on my desk
I am feeling light
bright
and focused
I am focused on escape
I sit on my bed
I force my hands through the hole in my gut
slide them behind my ribs
and pull out my heart
I put in a glass of water on the bedside table
I lie down and pull the blanket up to chest
I turn out the lamp
fix my pillow below my head
I pull out my eyes and drop
them in the crack between the bed and the wall
they fall and land amidst the
garbage my dog hides
I can finally sleep knowing I will
be free
when I drown in silence
tonight

Clenched Jaw Pack Of Smokes Pot Of Tea

I love you.

click

I love you.

click

I love you.

click

I love you.

click

Are you fucking kidding me?

I would never do this to you.

How could you?

I love you.

click

I love you.

click

I love you.

click

(it was always a dial tone with her)

Another Night In Oakland

Every time I go to a show my urges for violence get stronger and
stronger. I took the microphone tonight and mocked the drunken fools
in the crowd until they were spitting on me. Every time they spilled their
beer or pushed me I wanted to explode. My tolerance for their weak and
pathetic behavior is almost gone. I will destroy all of them.

Rest Stop

I used to run away and hide in the restroom to
cut
myself
and
punch
myself
now I go and run to the restroom,
cry
and
then wash my face.
This
is
growth?

Inside I Die

I know this thing
inside
it is violent it is
blind

I go these ways
I know these ways
now go away

I close my eyes
and go inside
It's where I
stay

I live now in this
place
I live down
and away

I know this thing
inside
it is violent it is
blind

I open my my eyes
and break the chains
see the sun again

I look down at
the grass it
is me
it, us, me

I know this thing
inside
it is violent it is
true

Bus Stop

A different bus stop
A different day
Same destination
Nowhere

Come

I cant come
unless I am listening to
Black Sabbath

Dreams Of Doubt

I had a dream that I kissed her
that we were together again
Everything was right
and beautiful
in my asleeping reality
there was no fear
or doubt
or worry
just decisions
I woke up and made my cup of tea

I was full of fear
doubt and worry
about my decisions
how long can wrong be ok?
when does the pain really set in at full
when does the pain fully set in for me?

(two honest lines were just erased
from ever being read)
but I don't need to worry, really, for
I can push these fears down pretty
deep

I can move on
just get through the day
until my head goes still
and I dream of her again

Dwelling

Every winter I get sick.
Well, almost every winter.
Some winters I just don't feel all that well.

Hostel

It started coming in flashes a few weeks ago
The windows breaking and the shrieking and crying of my little sister
I still haven't figured out what time it happened
Maybe mid afternoon
I had just gotten back to my house after ripping off my dealer
for a couple hundred bucks and a few bags
I think I was able to get high before I heard them pull up to the house
The next thing I remember is my mother getting me into the car
and we were heading to a hotel
The drive there was brutal
Mom Dad Rachel
all yelling and screaming
And I was just trying to hide from it all in my head
Things fade in and out in my head
I can see me getting high in the bathroom at the hotel
and I see me use in the parking lot while they are asleep
I remember the water burning me in the shower
I held my face under the steaming water as I cried
and screamed a scream that terrified my parents
It may have been 2 nights or a week
Its buried so deep in my mind
The last piece that fits
Is waking up at home a week or two after the rocks went through
our windows
I went to the front window to see if it was still raining
And they were standing in front of the house eating cereal
They just stared at me
I never told my family about that moment

Enter By Form Exit By Form

She is not familiar to me
   skin is not familiar
   eyes are not familiar
I am sure our feet have walked the
same streets
Our lungs are filled with the
same air
And that
Our skin is burned by the
same sun
But
She is not familiar to me

Again

I want to ask her if I can shut down.
It's so easy for me.
I want her to tell me it wont work,
that she doesn't want me.

But I don't want this to be the outcome.
I want her to reciprocate my feelings.

This place again, I cant believe it.
I am a weak creature.
I close my eyes and I don't see words like I normally do.
I see her. It kills me.
Maybe I will take a shortcut and just reject myself.
I don't need this obsession.
I need my thoughts back.
When I kill this off I will just get weak again and
someone else will infect my mind.
I like closing my eyes and seeing her.
That terrifies me.
I am a weak animal.
How much scar tissue will I need to build up to keep her out.
To keep me in.
I need to learn to keep this so deep inside that even I don't know
it exists.

Untitled Six

Sleep. I resent it. It has been out of reach for weeks. I get up every morning to legs that ache and eyes that are dry and burn. Spending 5 hours rolling around in a bed that won't get comfortable is getting old.

In the afternoons I start to get anxious. I daydream of having real dreams again. Just this morning I was in bed, kneeling over a pillow, punching it and screaming. The powerlessness of insomnia sets me on screaming rages. I punch and tear my pillows till my hands spasm and I collapse to the edge of sleep. It's on this edge that I can taste peace. I can smell it. But I cant get it into my stomach. I am so fucking hungry for it.

At times I wish for just 5 minutes. 5 Fucking minutes. I want to know what waking up is like again. I cant remember what the sensation of new and fresh light bleeding into my eyes is like. I am sick of hearing my thoughts bounce back into my ear from the sweat covered pillow I have my cheek against. Please let me drift away tonight. I will pretend I am part of a wave crashing onto the beach. I will go further and further into the horizon until I have buoys and boats on my shoulders. I would carry them, if only I had the energy.

Is Your Eyes

I was trapped.
To think, someday
"I will get out"

Well, I got out

but I still walk with a foot in the
grave

I can only get so far away
before I am living in the grip of Shame
again
Held down and tied off
Never thinking twice

It is lonely
at
the
bottom

It's amazing how long it took for me to
find
that out

But,
I
still walk hand
in
hand
with Shame
always looking back
Held down and tied off
Never having the time to think twice

I never thought twice.

Untitled One

As I sat down at my messy desk to write this
The Beatles' 'All You Need Is Love' came on
It destroyed anything I could have expressed here
I will leave my desk for my bed
I will go to sleep after taking my glasses off
My glasses that are smudged with her sweat and breath
I will tuck my hand beside my face and inhale her scent from
my fingers
Close my eyes, see her again and drift away

Everything and Everyone

Everything and everyone
seems to have
One
purpose
Break me
Kill me
and
Waste me

I lose my cool much to
easily
I just want to
Tear
and
Smash everything
and
Eve-
ryone
around me

My jaw hurts from
Biting my tongue
my arms ache
from restraining
My self

I imagine having
the freedom
to
Destroy everything

sometimes this
is the
only comfort I can find

that and
the thought of suicide
the thought
of
It
keeps me
going strong
the sheer acceptance of pain
and the will to endure it

the comfort does not come
from
the thought that
the pain
will someday be lifted

it is knowing that

I
Have
The
Power
To
End

It

All.

It eases a man to sleep.

Going Back

I would wait for you.
When you are ready
               for
               me,
I will
jump over mountains
nightmares and cities.
I will drop everything for you.
I am waiting.
Just call
and I will be there.

Fears

Easily flustered
Talking about writing
Set off
on a road that grows darker with every word
I try to respect my intent
I try
But I get so fucking angry
I don't want to explain
I like the fact that I am a natural cryptic
I just try to keep myself safe
but I fight it
I write into danger
judgment
and
acceptance

Take this,
I was out back and
he was telling me that I might
be cutting myself off with my coarseness
of language
not swearing
but the harshness of my tones and expressions

I told him to go put a gun in his mouth.

Understand,
accept
or die.

This is what it is
I am what this is
I am fear and gluttony
I climb high the walls of expression
and piss down all over the myself
as I look with knees trembling and stomachs knotted
at the crazy fuck about to jump (I am paralyzingly afraid of heights)

I Scream:
Jump you jerk off
Jump!
Just let yourself be known
by a few
just open up
to a few
I try
I try
I try to respect my intent

I can get pretty lost in self

Euhyme

He gets over on
everyone.
He is
lies.
thievery.
No matter what you
think,
and trust me,
every positive memory
you have of him
has been achieved through
smoke
and
mirrors
He is sick,
sick through and through
The one and only part of him
that is caring
cries
out,
begs
for
suicide.

I Came

Continue to
fly
and respond to
nothing

You are
above
You are
beginning
You are roots
You know everything
about
nothing

(ill)
(and)
(on)
(edge)

I Don't Want To Wait For It

Just fucking do it
Crack
Jump

All The God Talk Bullshit

I can hear her in the other room
when she comes in she will kiss me
and I will hide deep inside myself

Untitled Seventy

He always starts with what is visible
Erase and cut away
Rid

But this takes little time
And he is soon attacking
memory
and
fear

Fluidity Is Not To Be Found In This Place

Very quiet

I want to go on believing

But
during these times
I want to give up

on

everything

I see the end in front of me

My feet haven't quite touched the
ground
that
I
walk
on in a long time
I
am
lost
on a road far behind me

Now
I
only
seek
revelation
I am homemade
I am pipe-bomb

I walk
nothing
I say

I am over

I want enormous hospital bills
I want my house to burn down with itself in it

Repeating
in a tragic picture in mirror thingy

endless repercussions
battles lost
and lost

winners over here!

no

not there!

fools

marriage

sin

Ihate

Ijustwant

some

slowdowntimeformetoslowdownin

nowhere else to go

Fuck You Matt.

When I looked down and

saw what I was wearing,

black jacket

khakis

black boots,

I thought of you.

I wondered

Is this the last thing you saw before

you jumped?

Did you take one last look at the sky or the bay

before you?

Or

Did you close your eyes and then jump

having already seen enough?

because

You see nothing

now.

You are dead.

Fuck You Matt.

Happy With Life

I do not always echo like
　　this.
Sometimes, I am just repeated.
　　and dry.
I have spent many nights wrapped in
　　mistakes.
In the end I always pay for the
　　end.

Ever Depress A Waiter With Your Order?

I WANT NO SENSE
I WANT NO SENSE
BUT I MAKE SO MUCH OF IT

warp speed to shooting speed

I HAVE NO TIME FOR THIS

waste not want everything

I HAVE NOTHING INSIDE! willing to sell to
good home!

I HAVE NOTHING OF importance TO say

I did stop doing drugs/ I promise

prostitution, illegal????

Hey Boys, It's Fun Time

I KEEP FEELING LIKE I AM RUNNING OUT OF TIME
IF
I
MOVE
slower do I get more time to run out of?

time

breath

hair

friends

sight

teeth

hearing

books

I want to start finding things

but I want no part in searching

I want to blank stare myself into having everything

when I fail I want to be more upright than ever before

everything is desire

it is the only line

it is the only process of

thought

what can I get?
except pitiful weeping
maybe I don't have anything to give
I hope that
is it
I want more things to want

maybe if I give everything away I will
have more
space
time
energy
and wherewithal
to receive

I have an over abundance of desire
I am sick with need
I am filled to every brim with need
I want to want

Hundreds Of Times Over And Over

Again!
  you poor bastard
  No   wait   please   hold out for it
          come
                  skinned   knee........................please

    On!

Put your hand out
Have it slapped

Away
Again

Distrust
and
Disgust
my flavor.

"I'm not sad and I am not **really lonely**"
those like me have no feelings

I am SO different! and alone! its so dark in my
impenetrable closet humiliated isolation.

Hold me
Don't run
Love me
Don't run
I am so alone
and
I am broken again
unlovable

I really do hurt
I really am crying
I really am scared

do acknowledge it
and do not   tell anyone

I am an amerikan male
I work on cars and I hate fags
wait
wait
I AM NOT PART OF CONVENTIONAL MALE SOCIETY!!!

or am I?

TITS ASS

TITS ASS

TITS ASS

TITS ASS

TITS ASS

TITS ASS

TITS ASS

TITS ASS

TITS ASS

TITS ASS

TITS ASS

TITS ASS

TITS ASS

TITS ASS

TITS ASS

TITS ASS

TITS ASS

"All I wanna do is come in your mouth honey"

TITS ASS

TITS ASS

"YOU DISGUST ME! ALL MEN ARE PIGS AND RAPISTS IN WAITING!"

I'm not! I love and I care! I am just scared

oh, so scared ..

how should I feel
how should I feel
how should I feel
how should I know

I was given toy guns as a child
I kill
I
do
not feel

Not that I am strong
    I am weak but persistent
    I am a liar
    I am a junkie
    I am a thief

I am selfish
    and self seeking.
    the ideal mate
    love me

I am honest
I am caring
I am generous
I am loving

I am loved
the ideal tool
work me
over

Think
Betray
Love Care
Bleed and Come
We don't have a million years here
so lets go out into this wonderful world
and get hurt together.

Late Nightmare

I haven't slept in six days.

My saliva has turned a milky rust color and smells awful.

When I breathe through my nose I can smell my tongue.

I stand and begin to dry heave myself into a dizzy spell.

I am in a state of never ending confusion.

This

(what I believe to be) afternoon

I put my elbow through a closet door and a screw came loose

I picked it up and used it to scrape my gums off.

Watching my hands fill with something other than tears was shocking.

I am starting to find myself withering

and

howling,

rubbing my palms

over

my

aching

body.

I don't understand why this is happening to me.

I am a good boy.

Always be a good boy.
I'll be good.

I'm sorry.

Click

destroyed
destroyed
destroyed
destroyed
sometimes I hear this clicking in my head
and I can only hope that I will be
destroyed
destroyed
destroyed
destroyed
destroyed
destroyed
destroyed
destroyed
destroyed
destroyed
destroyed
destroyed
destroyed
destroyed
destroyed

Untitled Sixty

On the porch taking a break from boxing everything up. I hear people say that when they move, they "box their life up." Sounds like bullshit to me. My possessions are not my life.

There are two men down the street talking about weight loss down the street from me. "It is simple math, see, my wife wants to lose, well she is a buck 35 and wants to get down to uhh, a buck 30. She has her little program..." .

A truck comes from the hill beside them and turns into the men. I see them try to jump out of the way but it connects. The truck flips over and spills hundreds of turkeys and bricks of butter on them. I get up, light a smoke and walk around back so I don't have to see the mess that those two men were and are.

I Feel False All Over

Under
ground
High
ground

I chew myself raw
sad
idiotsee
idiotsaw

Special

Leave your body alone.

This skin!
The skin on my neck
is rubbing the wrong way
but it feels so
Good
Relaxing
Warm
Comforting
Strong

Enough to make me drop my smoke
Every tilt of my head is drawn out
and
silly

Roots

Honesty

Masks

Broken

Spending

Whipping

What am I fucking doing?

It is too bad I am

an

atheist

I

am

screwed

I Have Nothing To Bring To The Table

god
god
nothing correct
to look
at
anymore
everything
perfect
until
awoke
at ease
imperfections

spent
all
time
on
breathing
long
ago

when the time for anyones arrival is at hand
I will be asleep at the wheel

I

do not

want to be

part

of

this

damn game any

more

I am not free for you

I am not

free

to

do

this

any

more

I have given up my freedom

to

be

new

Joon

The thought of dying in a hospital bed terrifies me.
I want to die upon a mountain, underwater
To rot away in a field.
Food to all natures, glorious.
Founded in life and forever rooted in birth.
That is my dream. I want nothing more than to be the ground
I walk on.

Strong jaw.
Shaved Head.
Skirt.

Just being in public I feel unsafe.
I am ready for the attack.
I don't care anymore.
I am not looking.
You are welcome to attack at
anytime.

I have the music pumping loud.
Drown everything out.
I type with eyes closed.
If only the wind and sun
were not felt on my
skin.

Hey Pat

"Hey Rich it's _____. I was just calling to see how you are doing. I haven't seen you around lately and was worried. I wanted to let you know that I love you and you are special. Please call me soon."

When I heard this message I laughed. She has done nothing to show me over the years that she cares. There was a time when we were close but I guess I never flirted with her so I wasn't high on her list of priorities. I see her hanging around all these fucking lame scumbags and it saddens me. But hell, I don't give her what she wants me to so i'll receive these calls for awhile I guess and then hopefully she'll find something to numb the guilt of being a shallow cunt and she won't need to make these late night phone calls to me.

I Have Walls And A Roof

When things get heavy
I want to throw some shit into
a bag
and
disappear
Leave it all
Leave you all
behind
I am ok
With
everything
far behind
I can keep what
I want inside
Losing it
all
Leave it
all
behind

I look forward to
a day
when I am free
or desperate
enough
to rid
myself of everyone

Hell,
maybe
absolute
degradation
and
insanity
are the only things
that can lead me
to
trust
and
freedom.
I'm waiting.

Infect and Irritate

Cut off and removed
I will not destroy you-
you will wake up in
a strange world

I would love to
make you-
nothing
no more

Your wet bed
splintered shins-
rear ended
hornets nest in a bag

HHH

I can taste her on my lips
I can smell her on my pillow

It's All Downhill

as you were getting a glass of water

you started to feel it

you sat down immediately in the middle

of the kitchen

it was like you had just figured out the answer

to something that every fiber **of your being**

had been searching for

but in a sick way

it was like someone was vomiting on

every cell and atom **of your being**

you got up and your glass slipped out of your hand
and shattered beside a chair

you don't remember if you heard it break

but you do remember not having anything in your hand

and then looking down and seeing glass everywhere

you did not need water anymore

you needed a dark room

you needed music louder than your thoughts

you needed sleep

escape

you are sitting on your bed

unable to sleep

you don't want to be all alone with this

this pain or fear or sickness or whatever it is

you are too shocked by the suddenness of this pain

to take a moment to identify with or what is going on

you are just sick all over inside

waiting for the assault to end

Keep waiting.

January 14th, 4pm

Listening to Leadbelly and chain smoking

I am staring at a painting
Sometimes I just stare and am at a loss as what to do anymore

I don't remember doing this painting at all

I do blackout painting

I paint into and from a place of emptiness

Over.

Must run

I must hide

I am drowning in my own dream

clear

unhinged

narrow

devoid

void

void

void

I am hanging from my own rope this time

I am my end

I am my fault

I am not

streaming

spitting

strewn

enough is never enough

I am awake and unafraid

I am willing to change

I have not yet begun my growth

and I am already pained

straining

and

heaving

I will not choke on this breath

not just yet

come apart

come on

come and be smarter than god

god with a big g

god spelled out of fear

god drenched in my blood

god born on my sweat

I am now and forever away from thee

I have now broken my chains

and now I rest in my box

coffin does not entail end

end does not entail over

over is inhaled in my

sighs

I Disgust Myself

oh, and I sleep.

I Guess Mirrors Have To Be Broken In Like Shoes

I have always liked it this way
with cuts all over my body
my heart is the color
of

the color of
backs turned
being pushed

You
Have no clue

Erase
all
Progress

I
am
Afraid
to
Breed

I
am

drowning

On One Side

On one side of paper there
is a list of things to buy at the grocery store.
On the other side is a note that says:

"I can't do this anymore. I only brought pain and misery
to your lives. And Sarah, please take care of the cats. Love Mom"

The refrigerator and cupboards are empty
police find the body of a 38 year old Caucasian woman,
wearing nothing but a pair of corduroy shorts, dead of an apparently self inflicted gun shot wound to the chest.
She was lying on a pile of dirty laundry.
No cats were ever found.

Thanks

I could hear her soft footsteps going back and forth back and forth outside the bathroom door.

While cutting a hole into a travel mug I sliced my hand open and black-thick-blood came out

and dripped to the dirty and peeling tile floor. Her footsteps went away and I was alone to focus.

It was another afternoon and another day and another cut and another escape and another holiday locked away from my family.

I am trying to figure out what happened a few years ago on Thanksgiving at my Grandparents house.

I flash back to who I was and how I felt and what I saw and what I said but it comes and goes quickly.

I remember trying to make a pipe out of a travel mug and some rusty plumbing parts I found in the garage, being ok and then not being ok, and then I was locked in a bathroom with my young cousins trying to find me. I can still hear their little voices saying my name from outside in the hall.

I can still hear these voices even though I have not used drugs in five and a half years and I am alone on my bed listening to good music and feeling full from a good meal. I don't know why I try to figure out moments from my past.

I think the drive comes from me not being able to remember such large periods of my life. That is, I can analyze what I do recall, then maybe I can find out what has made me who and what I am.

Why would you try to figure out anything?

It should be no concern why or how but that it is.

(I will fight that voice as I continue)

My mother is sitting outside of the door now. She is crying and rubbing her hands on the door begging for me to come out. I continue to smoke and try to drown her out with dope. I thought I had enough weed to get me through the day but I was running out.

The fear that always hits when you are about to run out of drugs is paralyzing for a moment and then you spring to action. Use to live. Live to use. The closest I have come to feeling that since I have stopped using was a few months ago when I was almost hit by a bus.

She finally leaves and I sneak out to the room across from the bathroom and I start to dig in the closet for the stash I know I have hidden there. I cant find it so I go to the desk and I pull out every drawer and flip them upside down on the bed and I see the envelope that I am looking for.

Hiding my drugs was one of the sad miserable and many ways I attempted to control my drug use.

Only this much, Only on the weekends, Only with these people, Only if they buy it, Only in this combination. It never worked.

I can't believe its heroin. I am so fucked. I don't remember putting that there. But, its been so long, maybe a few months. This one day wont hurt me. I need to get foil and another lighter from the garage.

I look in the mirror and spit at my face. I scratch my throat to keep the scream down in my gut. They are having dinner now and my Mother wont come and make a scene. Now is the time to go outside.

I broke her heart that day. The look on her face as I walked by her and out the front door almost got through to me. Almost.

Back in the bathroom and asleep on the floor. I wake up with dried blood on my cheek. The envelope was enough to get me running.

The next few weeks are not anywhere to be found inside my head. I know that I went to San Fransisco and slept on the streets. The memories start to become clear a few weeks after the night at my Grandparents. I didn't go back there for 4 years. Next week will be my third Thanksgiving in a row. Now all I try not to do is yell at my uncle for being a racist prick.

Every night before dinner I have made sure to use that bathroom. To look myself in the eyes as I wash my hands. I can see the blood shot eyes. The dried tears. The scream. But now I see the dirt disappear from my hands and I dry them off and leave the room. I shut the door and I walk to the place where people say my name without fear or anger.

No Mom

In Spaceeee

(Totally unrelated to the piece that follows but seriously, fuck Elvis. I mean come on.)

impending

why

what we mean

it's the first time

that we meet each other

is in a dream

the blood

in our place

pretending

why

it seems

that we dream

Untitled Four

I was sitting under a street light with dry blood on my cracked lips

Losing consciousness to the sounds of the coyotes singing in the grass behind me

When I was a kid, I always thought the sounds meant they were trying to find eachother

Now I know it is just a pack of them tearing an animal apart

I just had the shit kicked out of me in Paul's garage by one of his tweaked out customers

I used to find something in that garage that made me feel like I found myself

Now I know it was just something that tore me apart

Spite

just fucking go
get your lips of of me
and go
it's not that I don't want
you
it's just,
I am finally in a place
where I don't need you
this is so new for me
and I want to live in my
new found freedom
for a bit

side note- I lasted about 4 days without her
called her for several days and gave up
freedom is overrated

aside from that note-
please fucking kill me

The Question

Write or
jerk off?
Bye.

I Saw Her...

I did

forget

the

night

I did not

lose

the

taste

of

her

Rat Inside

Sleep is not coming for hours but I know I will cry myself to it.

There is a violent and hot storm somewhere between my stomach

and lungs.

It becomes calm every few moments

and

then

it

screams and screams and screams.

I just want it to stop.

Stop.

Stop.

But I get weak and it tears me apart again.

And I weep and heave and scream and choke on fear.

Fear of myself.

Animal inside.

Weak animal inside.

Again I smile, again I laugh and again there is a reprieve.

But I see the numbness coming and I stare into the eyes

of

the

animal

in my chest.

And once more, I am raw.

I see my true reflection

when I meet the eyes

of the rat my

body is housing.

I am not afraid

of

being

destroyed from the inside out.

I wait for the day when my teeth

connect after chewing

through my lungs.

When the rat and I

sleep forever.

When the storm is calmed

forever.

When we kiss and make up.

When we both fall asleep

together, forever.

When our eyes are dry,

always dry.

.

Social Plan

Well, the poor sun is finally rising
and it is becoming more and more difficult to find words
in my tired little head.
My fingertips hurt from all the pounding
on this god damned typewriter,
my eyes burn
and every knife I reach for is so damn dull.
The Wagner record is skipping
and my bed is screaming for me.
I can no longer ignore its cries.

Good night.

I Was Then

laughed at and spit on

spoke

up

and shut

down

withered

and

torn

all

over

beaten down by a beaten path

crushed by

waves

of

uncertainty

his mother always turns her head when he

cries

out

he feels like

he feels like that

I feel like that

he is out of breath

I am out of breath too

he is driven out

I am driven out

we once thought we would make it out alive

we were foolish then

we know better now

Scratched Out Question Marks

When I was 8 9 10
I had the same nightmares
every night week month
I was alone on a porch
looking out at a chair
lit only by a street lamp
My sisters or
mother or
father
would be siting in the chair looking
at
me
An arm would come from
the dark
and strip them
of their clothes,
slowly tearing apart their
body
arms
legs
hair
stomach
Fuzzy
red clouds

I would wake up
sweating and screaming
My mother would be rubbing my back,
trying to whisper me to sleep

I realized
It was my hand
coming from the dark
It was my lips that kissed theirs into a
mute
scream
It
was
always
me

.

Shaking I Am Shit

"I am shit. I am shit, I am shit. They think I am shit. They all think I am shit"

Sitting on the porch with a box containing a chair in front of me
I have a small kitchen knife in my right hand
I use it to cut through the packing tape on the box
I get the mouth of the large box open
my hand starts to shake
there is snot dripping from my chin
I have been crying for several minutes
I have my teeth clenched
and am screaming through my teeth
"I am shit. I am shit, I am shit. They think I am shit. They all think I am shit"
"I am shit. I am shit, I am shit. They think I am shit. They all think I am shit"
"I am shit. I am shit, I am shit. They think I am shit. They all think I am shit"
"I am shit. I am shit, I am shit. They think I am shit. They all think I am shit"
"I am shit. I am shit, I am shit. They think I am shit. They all think I am shit"
I pause while cutting the tape............
I look at my left hand
It is calm.
It is safe.
It is controlled.
My right hand forces the knife into the palm of my poor, poor left hand.
I have snot dripping from my chin.
I am choking,

"I am shit. I am shit, I am shit. They think I am shit. They all think I am shit",
through a clenched jaw
and now I have blood dripping down the fingertips on my undeserving left hand.
I finish unpacking the chair and leave the porch.
I walk to my room.
I am sweating.
drooling.
screaming.
crying.
bleeding.
On my bed, I rock back and forth on the edge and say over and over and over
"I am shit. I am shit, I am shit. They think I am shit. They all think I am shit"
"I am shit. I am shit, I am shit. They think I am shit. They all think I am shit"
I see the dirty floor in front of me
there is my blood and spit on it.
In between my feet,
I see me.
I see myself in the filth *and* waste.

Out In The Cold I

Out in the cold I can feel what I hide from in the warmth.

I hold it in and see what it does to my hands, the way I stand.
I am always walking away.

People can force me only so far into a corner before
my will to care becomes will to survive.
I am not the person I have been for you all these years. I am
tearing
away. Far away.   Removed.

Again, I hold it in. I wash myself in the cool true air of the
midnight
walk.

Away.

You are no longer what I choose.
I am walking away.

The only warmth I crave is the scream of my skin against
the eyes of the night.

My Pores Ache From The War That Engulfs Me Please Someone Something Help Me

Sometimes

I

want

to

be

safe

but

at

other

times

I

feel

like

living

so

I

keep

on

crawling

She Always Calls At Inopportune Times

she says
I want to stop thinking
I say
that thinking is all I want
she says
I want to stop feeling
I say
well, I agree with you there
but I have no time for escapism
she says
I have no time for tragedy
I say nothing and hang up

Stealing

She scares herself.
She can't stop taking
what isn't hers.
She promises and screams and berates
"That's the last time, it won't
happen again, it just won't, don't worry,
all right! it won't, I won't!"
but sure enough...
She don't realize it until
confronted.
While stealing she does not remember the pain.
It doesn't come up at all.
I guess that is the scary part of it.
Every lie coming out,
trying to cover up
the fear and disgust inside.
Eventually, she admits her wrong
and earnestly pledges
to change.
Somewhere deep inside her gut starts to hurt
and churn and scream and burn.
She knows these promises won't stop her.
She can't stop herself.
She has no control.

Sweep

It was all gone

We were

lips

teeth   nails

hair

and

sweat

All ends were disappearing

scratching   laughing

   spent

All things were clouds and whistling

sweat hair lips nails teeth

Arms wrapped 'round bodies around legs

Tongues around necks

Fire

Fury

Heat

Release

We were cunt

We were cock

Everything soft was sweet

was nerves on end

were explosions

Pulling neck into throat

into swallow

into breath

Spinning rolling falling laughing

Cheek

Heat saliva

We were pulls

We were grips

We were all pressure

Then it evaporated into a soft sweet safe smile around us

We were

enveloped

Shitty Apple

God damn it

There is nothing like buying an apple and putting it in your bag.

Walking for 45 minutes to your house.

Washing the apple

and then biting into it only to find that it is rotten and diseased.

Indecision And Loneliness Guide My Hands

Unprotected sex
Followed by a day of wonder

Action is cure

Sitting

Just sitting alone in a creek.
He was walking when he realized that no destination
would ever be right for him.
He wonders where the nearest bridge is.
He wants to die in the water.
He dreamt of flying as a child.
He will jump.
That destination is
righteous.

I Put It In My Arm

It is not love that I put in my arm
It is escape
It is relief
It, unfortunately, is not forever

Sketches I Tell You I've Done

I am staring
at
my
face in the bathroom mirror
it is the only place that
no one
bothers me

if only I could leave my
self
outside
of
that
fucking
door

The Steam From The Cup Of Tea That Is Behind My Typewriter Is Warping The Paper

She is arriving at 8

I have been here since 6

I need these two hours to expel all the shit from me
so when she arrives I can speak her language

Something about communication terrifies me
I approach it like a war
plan strategies, hide and secure
my weakness

Some say just be yourself
Hell,
If they only knew

Smoke

Another morning smoke

I don't know what to describe here anymore

the bite of the cold concrete against the edge of my heel

or the shadow of the squirrel against the fence across the yard

I am surrounded by life and sensation

yet with every drag I take

I think about suicide

nothing grand or spectacular

just escape

from another morning like this

So Much Is Hidden And Seemingly Beyond Repair

Beyond realization

I looked
so deep inside that I
got
lost for weeks
When I emerged from self
I had lost my sense of imbalance

It is
Too bad that
I had thrown away everything
I had to hold on
to
long ago
Long ago

I would grab a hold of myself
if I had a self to grab a hold of

My hands are not safe
I lost trust in them
after all the
pain
they inflicted
upon
me

I guess I got smart
Now, I only have me to lose trust in

The only trust worth losing
is the trust you have in yourself.

I am driven to turn inside myself
To cut through the rot I have a fed on for so long
I dismantle

analyze
I run my hands in
to
dead ends
so much is hidden
and
seemingly beyond repair

Marie

She cant stop scratching and

watching her skin fall away

She is amazed at how it keeps coming and coming

When she feels the sting of the air hitting the new wound

She knows the blood is about to come

Her fingertips feel wet

She isn't scratching anymore

She is now digging

She pulls layers of her skin away

and the blood starts to mix with the pieces

of skin that have fallen on to

her uniform and the blacktop of the playground

She picks up a rock and puts it to the

place on her breastplate

where soft white skin used to be

She starts to tap it against the bone

this is a new sensation

She bounces the rock

against the wall of the violent place in her chest

She feels it click all the way down to her

heels

She begins to rub the rock against the wet bone

and soon she smells smoke

The cloud of dust burns her eyes

but she rubs and rubs and chisels away

until she feels a place of darkness and calm

She puts her hand into the place where
her heart would be
"It is empty" she says to herself
She smiles as she hears the bells ringing
and as she walks back to her class she
does not wonder how she will explain the blood
She knows she never has to explain anything
ever again
She is calm
She knows now that they
cannot hurt her anymore
That there is nothing for them to hurt
She only felt the pain because she was taught to feel it
Now she knows the
Truth

Untitled Sixteen

I am writing for one reason. I need to put something on this paper that is more dangerous than the poison that is in my head. Create some fucked up character so I can please just goddamn escape whats in my eyes for just a moment. Anything. Too many sentences are started and erased because they are too close to what I really think. And I don't think any mind but mine will ever or should ever understand this.

Who do I say any of this to?

I hate myself for feeling and thinking any of this sh:t.

Tea

We were sitting at a Japanese restaurant
and our orders came to us wrong so I used that as an excuse
and I left..
I did not pay for the shitty watery tea.
The three women I was with kept asking
me about how I was feeling.
I cant hide it from my face.
My posture says it all.
I lie and say I am just a bit tired.

As I am walking down the street a young boy
in front of two blue coolers asks me if I would like to
buy some juice. I say
No thanks, he offers soda.
I keep walking.

I get to the train station and try to buy a ticket
but my cash is fucked up and worn.
The machine rejects them.
I scream and I start to cry.
In front of all of these people.
I despise them.
I wipe my face with my sleeve and I inhale a painfully needed
breath of air.
I get my ticket, enter the platform and wait for the train.
One train, two trains go by and I imagine throwing myself in
front of both of them.
The first was a 6 car train so it stopped too short.
I would have been maimed and humiliated.
Not killed.
I wait for the next one that will arrive in 14 minutes.
I can feel the train crush me and then I feel the nothing.
I try to sit there and remember the pain and anger I was trying
to escape.
But nothing can come to my mind.
Sometimes having an imagination can truly keep you
from achieving your goals.

The train arrives. I walk in and find a seat away from people.
There are several stops till I get off so that means at least a 30 minute
opportunity for intrusion.
It doesn't even take one fucking stop for the assault to begin.
A woman sits next to me and immediately asks me about the book I am
reading.
I look at her and say I have just started it and that I have never read the author
so I have nothing to offer her.
She asks me if I am a writer.
I say I write.
She begins a sentence but i cut her off.
I say to her, "Before the line of questions I was someone who read." and then I
asked
if she would please "allow me to continue being that person."
I expected her to move but she stayed next to me.
I pretended to read for the next few stops until she exited the train.
10 minutes left.
I beg the god I do not believe in to please allow me 10 quiet minutes. 10
fucking minutes.

....this beautiful woman boards the train.
I continue to pretend that I am reading.
I toss my eyes up every few moments and slowly make my way
around her right ankle.
Up her thigh.
I look at and try to imagine the feel of her silk skirt against my hand.
I make my way to her hands.
She is holding a copy of Camus' Rebel.
I close my eyes and pretend she is talking to me about what the book means to
her.
She tells me about when she learned of the author in high school.
Over the next few months we become a sort of 2 man book club,
trading literature and meeting over good coffee to talk about our favorite
bookstores
and our fondness for the smell of old books.

Slowly we talk about our families, which leads to our fears and then to
the alarming anger we both direct towards everything.
I realize I love her and her anger and her silk and her ankles and I hate her
family
as much as she claims to.
As we are exchanging our wedding vows I faintly hear the conductor of the
train
say "Bay Point station is the end of line and the train is now out of service,
everyone must exit this train..."
I realize I have missed my stop.

I shuffle off and go across another lonely platform to wait for a train that is not
leaving for 11 minutes.
Again I see me in front of a train.
Again I feel relief and I lose touch with what I needed to escape from.
The time passes quickly and soon I am on an empty train.
No chance for anyone to invade my space.
I try not to think of her, to force myself to think that in just a few moments I
will be out of
this metal box and my shoes will be hitting the concrete as I make my way
home, again.
In just few short moments I am putting my ticket into the turnstile and my
shoes touch the sidewalk.

In the cold breeze of the evening I find it hard to to remain hidden from whats
inside me for any length of time.
I feel the breeze coming from the cars as they speed past my fragile and
vulnerable body.
It wouldn't take much more than a compact car going a little to fast for the road
to turn me into a stain that will wash away in the coming winter rains.
I am now in front of the golf course and I can smell the freshly cut grass.
The air is heavy with something wet, I look and I can see that the sprinklers are
on.
Rarely do cars come speeding down this stretch of road this time of night.
I guess that soon I will be in my bed drinking my perfectly brewed tea.
My imagination is the reason I am alive for another night.
No cars have passed me and I am at my front door.
My dog is barking as I insert my key into the lock.
He jumps off of the couch and greets me as I drop to my knees.

I let him lick my face.
This is real. This is real.
I often repeat this to myself in different variations.
I don't want it to to be real, but I really am in bed alone and dreaming of her.
All of the hers.
I spill tea and it burns my wrist.
It wakes me up a bit.
I fall asleep shortly thereafter.

The Other Hundred And Fifty People

I am upside down.

Vomit is filling my lungs.

I am finally alive.

Thank you.

I am running this show now.

Trainwreck Homewreck

What was

I think I to know

I guess I don't have my disposal lately

I am even running out of words

I have not been time

not out of fear…

…just

….I have seen myself enough to know when to quit

I fallen over the finished line a few times

of

of avoidance

detainment

lover flown coop

roles

reels

cut

raped by all sorts of dope

I have seen the way I look at me

I am not good enough

I am just not enough

when I awoke and found everything 'round me in ruins
destroyed
by
hypocrisy
mockery
and oaths
dirty shirts and dirty dreams
detachment
entertainment

bird on the wire checked into rehab again

truth is on vacation
sincerity is on paid sick leave
apply
apply
apply
apply
apply
apply
apply
catharsis
insane
and unsafe
apply

Untitled 2

she sat down at my table
intrusion
when she left
she nuzzled her face
into my neck
shivers erupted throughout
my
body
I felt real warmth
for the first time
in
weeks

Untitled 5

She was sitting in front of me
crying.
I left the room to go have a
smoke.
When I returned she was not
there.
She had forgotten her large green
purse.
I picked it up and brought it to the
restroom.
Sitting in a stall I opened it and
smiled.
It was full of pill bottles and
make-up.
I left the bathroom feeling great, looking
great.

Waiting For The Blast

The moment after I ask a question

while she

inhales

and I

digest

the look on her face

Is

eternity

Is

suffocation

I do not have time to

swallow

the saliva

that my words

swam through to

get out

of my chest

before she

shoots

me down

I am always walking

away

Waking Up

When I was using drugs I woke up every morning feeling exactly the same. There was no escaping the shame. I went to sleep in fear and woke up in pain. But now everything has melted into one long yawn.

People do not know how tired I am because I can hide everything behind a smile. At least I am not bothered by the questions that occur when one walks around with a yawn plastered on his face. I don't need sleep. I need relief. I need a reprieve, a moment, a lifetime. I need to escape the regret. Although, I do understand this is much too much to ask for.

We Are Mountains

We are mountains.
We are names.
We spit out the entire sea
and create the sky within our wake

We are heavens sake.

We are information.
We are birth.
We drink up all sunsets
and create stars with every breath

We are nothing, more or less

Wondering

Did a show last night in SF

cleared the place out

What I do is the opposite of what people

want to hear on a Saturday night

After the show I went and watched a meteor shower

with a few people

in the hills of Berkeley

At first, I couldn't see beauty in the sky

and I wouldn't see beauty in the lights of the city below

After awhile this changed

I stayed on the hill with Ellen until I couldn't handle the

clouds or stars or silence anymore

I think I slept for 2 hours last night

I am sitting on Shattuck about to get up and walk to the campus to

see Kyla perform in a play

I feel like a corpse

The coffee has already faded from my muscles my heart

my mind

I have to go now

If you want to see a dead man walk across town

Now is the time

Untitled 3

I fall so far

my dreams are too high

but

it's hard not to keep them

that

way

when you feel

so

I Left There Wanting To Die

Object to object.

Untitled 4

green ribbon tied around her ankles
piercing in her bottom lip
scars of motherhood on her stomach
fire in her smile
permanent moans
nail-polish worn away on her fingertips
even this
beauty will someday die
will become dust
decay
makes one wonder if anything is really
worth the trouble

Work

I left for work early this morning so I could stop and get coffee.
Sitting outside were a few people I know in passing. An old man
named Jim was there telling stories of his boxing career in the
forties. "Never knocked out" he kept saying. I believe him. He
is a tough ol' fucker.

The other few guys sitting around where just wasting breath and
ogling women. I smile and laughed on the outside. I don't need to
let them know how sick they make me. A car was driving erratically
and I was hoping that it would wipe them and their table out. It kept
going and going and going and then it was gone. They were left sitting
and talking shit.

Around 11 I headed towards work and left them and their noise behind me.
The people I work with are ok, I guess. .

Writhe

I am walking in a brightly lit hallway.

Every corner I come upon is never fully realized.

I can not turn what does not materialize.

I walk quickly and throw my eyes around to find my way (out or into somewhere).

I catch a look at my forearms.

They are covered with large worms.

I shake my arms about and try to brush them off but they scream at me and I stop.

I sit down.

I stare at my hands.

I can't figure out if the worms are destroying me or if they are creating me.

I look up and I am at a dead

end.

You

That damn piano line is all I can hear sometimes.

Pause
it wasn't me
it was you
Yes
think about it
I just sat there
and you were up there
I understand it,
what it's like to hide
on another planet
but don't blame me
it was you
not me
i'm still sitting here
not waiting
but i'm still here
sitting next to animalism
resting my head on laughters
shoulder
see,
laughter knows it was you
and not me

interrupted.

Committed To No Part Of My Life

I don't

Have
To
Be
In
Pain

to write

I just
usually
happen
to

Be
In
Pain

But, Little To Lose

Parliament on the box
smoke in hand
tea brewing
rain falling
beauty
sensuality
my senses are alive
and I am beauty

Somehow I Will Find Out

The tea burns my throat and is cleansing

If only what I scream could be that powerful.

I try screaming

but I can barely hear myself,

at least not enough to drown the fear out.

I Am Going On

Thoughts
and
Gross
are dripping outta my right ear
everything is covered in water
my paintings
my tapes and books
everything but my typewriter
nice for me
this is alright with me
I'll be ok tonight

I Have Spine

And

I

Want

To

Cease

To

Exist

Narcotic Raped Blood

My right
pointer finger
aches at night
from assaulting
this keyboard
it feels
burned
out

Privelege

White woman
slam
Black woman
slam
White woman
slam
Black woman slam
slam
white woman
slam
black woman
slam

slam
woman
slam
woman
slam
woman
beat her head
slam woman
slam slam slam slam
woman
fall
woman
crush woman
slam woman
penetrate woman
slam slam slam slam
woman

step
on
woman
woman cry
woman bleeds

man
walks away
whistling
happily

Thank You For All The Kind Words

Avoid

A void

Afterbirth

Its 6 am
the glow in the dark
inverted cross
above my bed
is fading
and I am ready for
my day
to
begin
I'm going to go shower
jerk off and smoke
breakfast of champions

Sir, Goodbye

I
always
wanted
to
be
like
you
but
now
I
know
and
accept
my
place

Heart Stone Hearts Tone

It is not normal for
me to accept love
it is a muscle
it is a decision
it is a stone

Write Smoke Write

Eating greasy left over chinese food
trying to enjoy what is utterly
unenjoyable
the phone wont stop ringing
and a shitty movie is on T.V.
I want to bury myself in my backyard
but it is raining
and I hate to get wet

Suck Machine

Seeing you trying to fit into
a culture that rejects you makes me
so sad
Losing weight for an audience
Jerking off beasts in neckties

Why don't you put energy
into changing it?
Rather than losing you

I can not come to your shows anymore
It hurts to see the selling of my friends
I cant watch this
I will not sit and watch
Watch you sell out and disappear

I used to be thrilled when you played
but now I see that you are the ones being played

Do you really not see what is going on?
Do you not care anymore?
Burn the contract

Fuck the record off
Please come back to us
Lose the suits
Lose the suits

Empower our young woman
Stop fattening the suits' wallets
They could use some thinning
not you

Break the chains and be free with us again
There is only so long before you are stuck forever
Please break away and be real again

I know you think your image is of a strong woman
asserting her will in a world
run by pig men

But you are just what they want you to be

Willing to run it off for them
You're suckers

They have sucked you in

Big tours

Big money

They cant fill the place where your integrity once lived

I am going to miss you

Is Mommy Helping You Build?

They always leave
me
crushed.

Burned out,
spiteful,
and crushed.

www.ingramcontent.com/pod-product-compliance
Lightning Source LLC
Chambersburg PA
CBHW031606260626
47154CB00020B/1640